Polar Bear Bowler

for Christopher F
Christopher William
& Christopher James

Karl Beckstrand

Ashley Sanborn

Polar Bear Bowler / Polar Bowlers
A Story Without Words Vol. I
Vol. II: Butterfly Blink

Premio Publishing & Gozo Books
Midvale, UT, USA
Library of Congress Catalog Number: 2014947746
ISBN: 978-1503388673, eISBN: 9781311262097
Text Copyright © 2014 Karl Beckstrand
Illustration Copyright © 2014 Ashley Sanborn

ORDER direct, or via any major distributor. Libros online books FREE/GRATIS:
Premiobooks.com

Other books/ebooks by Karl Beckstrand:
The Bridge of the Golden Wood: A Parable on How to Earn a Living
Horse & Dog Adventures in Early California: Short Stories & Poems
Ma MacDonald Flees the Farm: It's not a pretty picture ... book
She Doesn't Want the Worms! – ¡Ella no quiere los gusanos!
Crumbs on the Stairs – Migas en las escaleras: A Mystery
No Offense: Communication Guaranteed Not to Offend
Sounds in the House – Sonidos en la casa: A Mystery
It Ain't Flat: A Memorizable Book of Countries
The Dancing Flamingos of Lake Chimichanga
Bright Star, Night Star: An Astronomy Story
Arriba Up, Abajo Down at the Boardwalk
Bad Bananas: A Story Cookbook for Kids
Butterfly Blink: A Book Without Words
Great Cape o' Colors - Capa de colores
Why Juan Can't Sleep: A Mystery?
Muffy & Valor: A True Story
To Swallow the Earth
Anna's Prayer
Ida's Witness

Multicultural Books
by PREMIOBOOKS.com

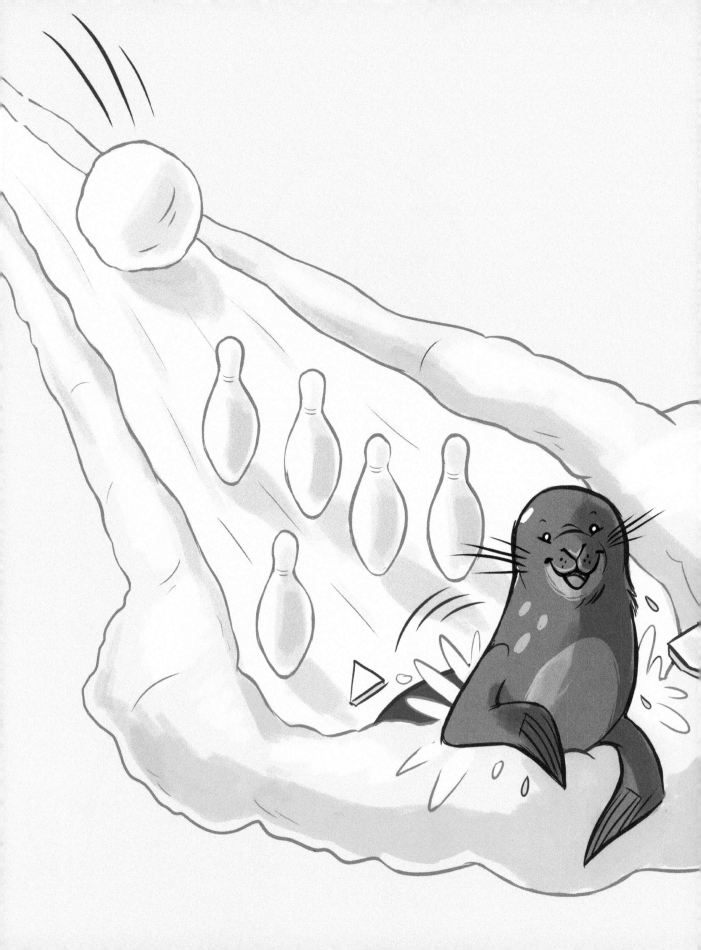

CPSIA information can be obtained
at www.ICGtesting.com
Printed in the USA
LVHW07*0124120418
573026LV00004B/12/P

9 780985 398835